Knight Time

Jane Clarke and Jane Massey

RED FOX

In the time of the knights,

it was (k)nighttime again.

Little Knight and Little Dragon

Their daddies read
them a story,

were getting ready for bed.

tucked them into bed
and kissed them
goodnight.

And then their daddies went out.

It was a night for nightmares
and things that go bump in the night.

Their rooms were full of **scary shadows**.

"I want my daddy!"

they cried.

But their daddies were in the forest,
and the forest was very dark
and very,

very . . .

Yes! Their daddies held them tight.

But . . .

Do knights have scales?

Do dragons wear armour?

NO!

"Please don't eat me!" Little Knight
and Little Dragon cried, at the very same time.

"I don't eat knights," said Daddy Dragon.

"I don't eat dragons," said Daddy Knight.

"Then why do dragons hunt knights, and knights hunt dragons?" the little ones asked.

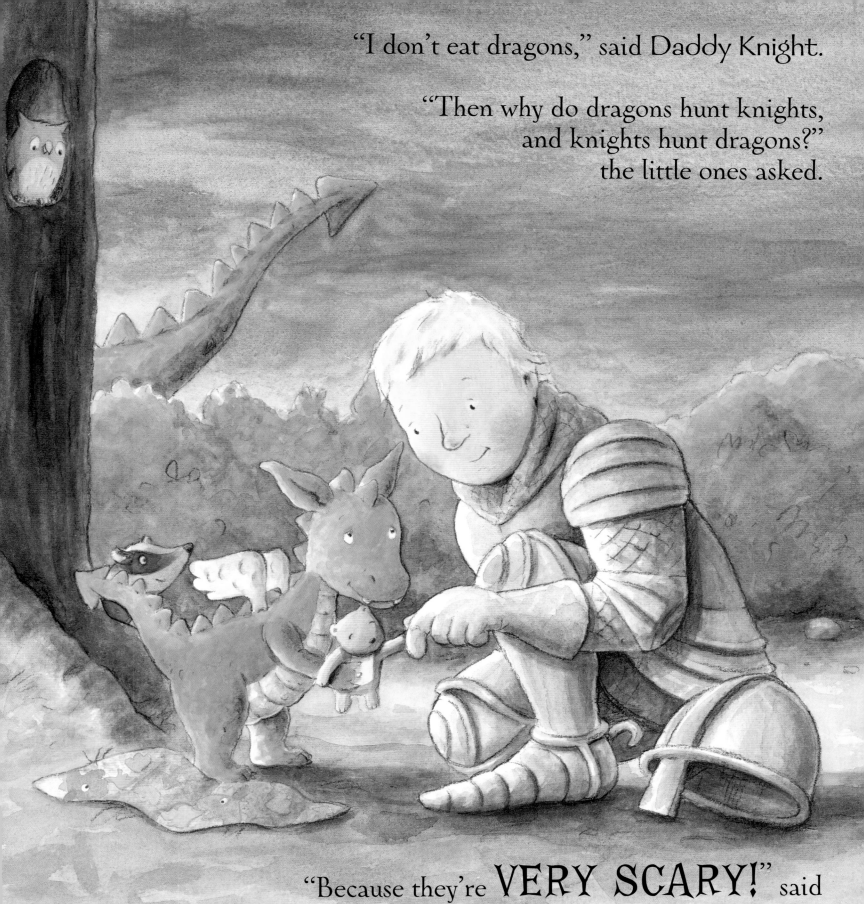

"Because they're VERY SCARY!" said their daddies, at the very same time.

Little Knight looked at Little Dragon's
teddy bear and blanket.
"You're not that scary!" he said.

Little Dragon looked at Little Knight's
teddy bear and blanket.
"You're not that scary, either!" he said.

"Then it's silly to hunt each other,"
Little Knight and Little Dragon told their daddies.

"But we always hunt each other at this time of night," their daddies wailed. "Whatever are we going to do?"

"You could try to be friends," said
Little Knight and Little Dragon, "like us!"

So from then on,

the time of the knights was a lot more fun . . .

. . . and (k)nighttime was lovely and peaceful.

Sweet dreams, everyone!

For Dennis – JC
For the Trevor Mann Baby Unit and RSCH, Brighton - JM

KNIGHT TIME
978 1 4351 4981 6

First published in Great Britain by Red Fox,
an imprint of Random House Children's Publishers UK
A Random House Group Company

This edition published 2013

Lot #: 1 3 5 7 9 10 8 6 4 2

RANDOM HOUSE CHILDREN'S PUBLISHERS UK
61-63 Uxbridge Road, London W5 5SA

THE RANDOM HOUSE GROUP Limited Reg. No. 954009

A CIP catalogue record for this book is available from the British Library.

Manufactured in China
05/13